Violet Bing

and
The Grand House

Jennifer Paros

Viking

Much gratitude to Catherine Frank for helping
Violet Bing and Jennifer Paros get from here to there
safely. Special thanks to Max Kenower for all his strength
and perceptions. Much appreciation to Sawyer Kenower
for his open heart. And for WDBK: thank you.
I adore you, as always.

VIKING
Published by Penguin Group
Penguin Young Readers Group, 345 Hudson Street, New York, New York 10014, U.S.A.

Penguin Books Ltd, Registered Offices: 80 Strand, London WC2R 0RL, England

First published in 2007 by Viking, a division of Penguin Young Readers Group

1   3   5   7   9   10   8   6   4   2

LIBRARY OF CONGRESS CATALOGING-IN-PUBLICATION DATA
Paros, Jennifer.
Violet Bing and the grand house / by Jennifer Paros. — 1st ed.
p. cm.
Summary: Very definite in her likes and dislikes, seven (nearly eight)-year-old Violet Bing
goes to stay with her unusual Great-aunt Astrid in the Grand House.
ISBN-13: 978-0-670-06151-8 (hardcover)
[1. Great-aunts—Fiction. 2. Dwellings—Fiction. 3. Friendship—Fiction. 4. Curiosity—
Fiction. 5. Self-confidence—Fiction.] I. Title.
PZ7.P2434Vio 2007
[Fic]—dc22
2006010199

Manufactured in China
Set in Bembo
Book design by Kelley McIntyre

For Those Who Don't Get Out Much
But Who Really Ought:
The world is waiting for you.

* Contents *

* 1 *
Here Is Violet Bing

On a day that feels like a Sunday but is really a Monday, sometime between breakfast and lunch, Violet Bing, who is seven, almost eight, announces that she will *not* be going on the family vacation. On this day, Violet's parents say, "You must go."

But Violet will not go.

Saying "no" is not uncommon for Violet. She has said "no" to pancakes because they were bumpy; she has said "no" to swimming, to piano, to going over to someone's house, and to eating out, but never to anything this big.

"Think of it as an Adventure," her parents say.

Violet thinks that an Adventure requires a person who wants to find out what happens next, and she does not. If she was a different type of person, the vacation idea might work. For instance, if her name were not Violet Odelia Bing, but something else, she could probably go. But she hasn't found the right name yet. She would like the new name to be great. With the new name, she hopes she will be able to wear her hair in a ponytail without taking it down right away because it feels uncomfortable. As it is now, with the  name "Violet," she just can't feel comfortable with a ponytail or a vacation.

Also, she has many things to do and think and doesn't feel she has the time for anything else. When Violet looks up "time" in the dictionary, it says, "every moment there has ever been or ever will be," but it still seems like there isn't enough.

And so, these are the reasons Violet Bing says "no" to the family vacation. But before this can be over, she has a few more things to say first.

"I don't want to go *anywhere* or do *anything*!"

But she knows this is not the truth. She thinks the truth is probably more like this: "Sometimes I don't want to go anywhere and sometimes I do, but mainly I'm against Surprises and Things I Don't Know." In order to keep her point clear, Violet decides not to explain.

Her parents say, "Well, it's off to stay with your great-aunt Astrid at The Grand House unless you say 'yes.'"

She doesn't even know her great-aunt Astrid, but Violet will never say "yes."

Here Violet sets to packing. She has her own sort of system. There's a lot of throwing involved. Packing doesn't necessarily have to be *neat*, and Violet knows this. Although most people do fold things first, Violet is not interested in what most people do.

Her parents drive her to The Grand House.
Violet sits in the backseat with her brother.
The ride is long and everyone wants her to
change her mind. After some debate, however,
they give up. Now the ride is long and *quiet*.
She stares out the window and wonders what
will happen next.

Here is Violet saying good-bye to her parents and her brother. There is a wave but no hugs. Her parents stay in the car as Violet insists upon walking to The Grand House by herself. However, the walk up the pathway is dusty and hot, and she is tired and carrying her suitcase, which has many important— and some heavier, not-so-important—things

in it. For instance, Violet may find, upon arriving, that she has forgotten her toothbrush but remembered her dictionary.

The path winds and seems to go on indefinitely. Finally she comes to the steps of The Grand House.

✳ 2 ✳
Introducing The Grand House

Here is Violet greeted by her great-aunt Astrid. To Violet, the house hardly seems "Grand" at all—just *old* and *big*.

"Welcome, Violet Bing. It's about time we should meet!"

Astrid leads Violet down a hall, past lamps, pictures, rugs, vases, candlesticks, breakable things, and things that are appealing because they're big or old or complicated looking.

Violet walks past without stopping to look at
or touch anything.

"I'm thinking," says Astrid, "that because
the day is still so young, we might pack a lunch
and go out."

"I don't have time," says Violet.

"Of course, we can always have something to eat here."

Violet says, "I'm not hungry."

"Perhaps our first order of business should be the house," says Astrid. "When I first met this house I did not like it. So I want *you* to have a *proper* introduction."

Violet imagines being introduced to a house: "Violet, this is House. House, this is Violet. You two should have a lot in common."

"Right now," continues Astrid, "we're in the Kitchen. Around the corner—the Living Room, Second Living Room, and Ballroom. *Every* room holds Something of Interest. Things I want to think about, do, or study. Things of Interest can be anywhere or anything, but they *must* make you want to know more."

Violet thinks, *Aunt Astrid talks a lot.*

"On the Second Floor are all sorts of other rooms such as the Library—a world of books I—"

"Too much to read," says Violet.

"And the Fish Room, based on my great interest in the ocean—"

"I can't swim."

"The Hat Room—interesting things you can wear—"

"Hats make your head hot."

Violet does not actually know if this is true, but it seems likely they would.

If it is cold, she thinks, *then a hat could be of use; if it's warm, then it would be too hot. Some people wear hats in summer. But if you wore a heavy woolen cap in summer then it would make your head too hot. But then, wearing the wrong thing at the wrong time cannot be proof that the thing itself is wrong. The truth is long and hard to get right.*

Summer floppy

knitted and itchy

ear flaps

"There are many other rooms as well," continues Astrid. "The This and That Room, the Writing Room, the Bells and Baubles Room, Conversing, Navigation, and of course, the Basement, which is straight ahead."

14

Violet looks and sees the door marked
BACK STAIRS TO THE BASEMENT.

"Perhaps," says Astrid, "the Basement
would be a good place to start."

She opens the door. The banister is old
but still steady, the steps crooked but stable.

They pass books, old furniture, two sets of washers and dryers, an antique sewing machine, boxes, plastic bags filled with other plastic bags neatly saved, plastic bags filled with paper bags, and plastic bags filled with rubber bands. And up against the wall, in the corner, is an old BICYCLE.

Crossing the room, Astrid leads Violet to the BICYCLE. Although it is dusty, Violet can see that the BICYCLE is **red** and has no training wheels. At home, she has her own bicycle, but it is not **red**. And although this BICYCLE looks very old, she likes it better than the blue bicycle with the white stripe and training wheels she got as a surprise that

is too high up and hard to pedal. She does not like the training wheels because she is too old to ride with training wheels and so she does *not*. Meaning she does not ride at *all*, really, and is not sure she knows how.

Astrid picks up a cloth and wipes off some of the dust.

"Perhaps," she says, "we could fix it up a bit, make a sandwich or two, and take a ride to the Ocean today. I believe the Ocean is one of the best places a person can go. And you could go swimming as well. What do you think?"

Violet thinks she likes her sandwiches with white bread that is nice and soft. She

likes them to have the smooth kind of peanut butter and not too much of it, and her jelly must be grape because sometimes strawberry has *pieces* of strawberry in it. And also, along with not being all that good at riding a bicycle, she can't swim because she does not want to put her face in the water. Putting her face in the water seems like a bad idea because you cannot breathe while your face is in the water.

Violet says, "No thanks. I don't have time."

* 3 *
The Yellow Room

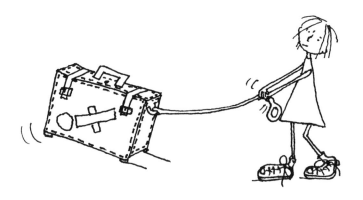

After leaving the Basement, they continue with their tour of The Grand House. Down a corridor, around a corner to a door marked BACK STAIRS TO THE SECOND FLOOR they go. Here is Violet putting her suitcase down, picking it up, dragging it, lifting it, carrying it with both hands, with one, with help, by the strap, by the handle. Past the This and That Room, the Library, and the Conversing Room, they go down another corridor, around another corner to a door marked BACK STAIRS TO THE THIRD FLOOR.

"You can choose one of these bedrooms as your own," Astrid says, pointing out the

first room. "There is the Orange Room—"

"I don't like oranges," says Violet.

"The Green Room?"

"Some people find green eerie."

"The Yell—"

Violet shakes her head. "It's like those songs at school where they make you clap along."

"Red, brown, blue?"

"No."

"Purple?"

Violet shakes her head. "Color is fine on something like a flower or a dress, but not on rooms. Rooms should be white."

This statement does not seem true either, which leaves her uneasy and wondering how she can ever say anything that will come out right. She nudges the suitcase with her foot; her hands are sore and her arm aches from carrying it. *And* she's tired from all those stairs. Why put so many steps in a staircase?

In the end, although it is possible a room should *not* be a color, one must be chosen. Her suitcase is placed in the Yellow Room, and Violet sits down on the bed. Up against the brightness of the room, Violet feels dark.

Astrid suggests they start preparing dinner.

"I have to go to sleep."

It is four thirty in the afternoon.

"I see. Well, if you wake and find you are hungry or suddenly have time, please call out. I'll be glad to hear from you. Good night, Violet Bing. Do remember to keep an eye out for Things of Interest; they are *so* easy to miss and often of the greatest help."

Violet says, "There *is* nothing of Interest," and, "I want to go home."

"If that's true, don't worry—I will not stand in the way of what must be done, although I was much happier to see you arrive than I will be to see you leave."

Violet watches as Astrid closes the door behind her. It isn't really true that she wants to go home. However, it seems to her that the truth here could get very long, and that it is much shorter to tell only a part of it. Violet decides to unpack and not think about it anymore.

Violet doesn't have much of a system for *un*packing, but her approach turns out to be similar to her system for *packing*. Look at all

of her things on the floor. She finds her nightgown, puts it on, and crawls into the big yellow bed. She closes her eyes to the *lemon, banana, mustard, sunflower, daffodil, yellow-rose* of the room's furniture, curtains, and lamp shades. But there are too many pillows and the comforter is very thick and her body disappears, leaving only her small face resting against the pale *cotton grapefruit* of the pillowcase.

She thinks, *It's like I'm drowning in Bright.*

* 4 *
The First Days
or How Violet Catches a Dog

For the next few days, Violet spends a great deal of time sitting in the large yellow chair she pushes over to the window of her new room. She stares out looking mostly at things she has already looked at before: the green grass, the large tree, the circle of tulips beneath the tree, the bench nearby, occasionally the sky, and the path that winds around The Grand House and eventually leads to the stone road.

There isn't much to say about what Violet does, for she doesn't do much. She does make

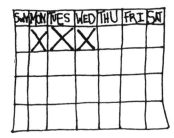

a calendar and place large Xs through the days she has been at The Grand House. When she is through putting Xs, she will go home.

Aunt Astrid invites her to do things, make things, see things, or go places, but Violet always says, "I don't have time."

"Well, perhaps soon you will have time," says Aunt Astrid.

One day after having placed her third X on the calendar, Violet goes to sit down in the yellow chair and spots something different outside. It is a girl, about her age, wearing a long strand of beads and carrying a picnic basket. First the girl wanders up the path and down again, then steps behind the large tree. For a moment, she disappears and then returns, crouching down and looking behind some bushes. Violet pulls her chair closer to

the window. Sometimes the girl wanders off to the left, sometimes to the right. Violet hopes the girl might open the picnic basket, but she never does. Then, after searching the same places again, the girl does something unexpected. She looks up and spots Violet in the window.

"Hi!" she calls out, waving.

Violet holds up a quick hand in return and starts to move away from the window. "Have you seen a dog?" the girl asks, still carrying the picnic basket.

Violet shakes her head.

"I'm looking for a dog," shouts the girl. "Have you seen him? He went this way."

"No," says Violet.

"You want to help look?"

Violet is about to say "no"

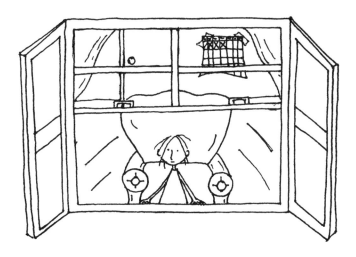

when she spots a dog running along the path toward the front of The Grand House. But before she can point, the girl sees him, too, and starts running, slowed considerably by the picnic basket.

Now Violet runs, too. Out of the Yellow Room and down the steps in order to get a better view through another window. But by the time she's gone down all the steps, she can't see anything through any of the windows and runs for the front door. Turning the handle as quickly as she can, she throws the door open and stands at the threshold, staring out. There, at the edge of the porch, is the Dog, sitting quietly. Just then, the girl approaches, quite out of breath.

"Quick," she says, "you grab him and I'll open the basket!"

But just as Violet thinks, *I'd rather be the one to open the basket,* the Dog looks at Violet, walks over, and licks her hand.

"You caught him!" announces the girl. "You caught him!"

And that is how Violet Bing catches the Dog.

* 5 *
Four Good Names

Maggie   Nolie   Goldie

Violet soon learns the girl's name is Magnolia Greene Gold—but she can be called "Maggie," "Nolie," or "Goldie," as she explains it, and likes her name because of its versatility. Violet thinks Magnolia is lucky to have four names she likes when Violet doesn't even have one.

Maggie explains that the same thing can be done with "Violet Odelia Bing."

"You can be 'Letty,' 'Odie,' or 'Delie.'"
Violet wishes she could like one of these.

Letty

Odie

Delie

Also, Maggie *made* the beads she is wearing—out of papier-mâché.

"Do you want them?" she asks, touching the necklace.

Violet actually does like them but does not wear beads.

"No thanks."

Then Magnolia has to go because it's time for lunch. She will be back once her parents

say she can keep the Dog, which she hopes
they will. Then she tells Violet not to name
him without her. Violet looks over at the
Dog and thinks he looks too smart for a
name and she wouldn't know what to call
him anyway. *He should call himself whatever
he wants,* she thinks.

"Bye, Violet Bing," Magnolia says, picking
up her picnic basket. "See you when I see you!"

And at that, Violet closes the door and is
left alone with the Dog.

The Dog follows Violet into the Kitchen.
And when she sits down, he sits down next
to her, very close to her chair. And when she
goes to push her chair out, he hardly moves
and she bumps his legs.

"Sorry," she says, looking at him for a
moment.

He lays his head on her lap and closes his eyes while she eats her sandwich, drinks her milk, and finishes two cookies.

Aunt Astrid says, "He may be hungry, as well."

Violet starts to stand in order to get him something to eat when she realizes he is

asleep on her leg, and she slowly sits back down. She doesn't know much about pets; she's never owned one and has never taken much of an interest in animals. After a while, Violet gently lifts the Dog's head, intending to put it onto the chair. But before she can do this, he awakens. She makes him the same lunch she had and hopes this will work.

After he finishes his last cookie, they go up to the Yellow Room to look out the window. The Dog takes to the big yellow chair. He sits on the armrests or sometimes squeezes himself onto the seat beside Violet. After a while, Aunt Astrid comes in.

"You know," she says, observing the Dog, "we will need to walk him."

Violet looks up at her.

"But if you don't have the time, I understand. I can always do it."

"No," says Violet, looking back out the window, "I think I have time."

"Oh, good," says Astrid.

After giving Violet a kiss on the cheek and scratching the Dog's ears, which he likes very much, Aunt Astrid leaves. Violet looks at the Dog. Lifting her hand, she tries petting him the same way and finds he likes it when she does it, as well.

* 6 *
The Truth about Being Busy
or Magnolia Greene Gold Comes Back

When Magnolia Greene Gold returns early the next day, she says, "I can't keep the Dog. Can I see your room?"

Violet walks Maggie up the two flights of stairs and down the hallway to the Yellow Room.

As it turns out, even though he's a stray and she would take good care of him, her parents won't let her keep the Dog because they don't actually *want* a dog. Aunt Astrid, who overhears the conversation, feels there is room at The Grand House for the Dog.

"Ooh," Magnolia says, "my room's light blue. Is your room at home yellow, too?"

"No."

"I painted my room myself."

This interests Violet.

"And then I moved my bed under the window, so I could look out, and the dresser to the other wall and my desk near the door."

Violet and Magnolia talk for quite some time. And in the Living Room and in the Second Living Room, they have races where they crawl on only one hand and one leg, or roll on their sides—which is challenging on a flat surface—or slither. These are all Maggie's ideas.

Then Magnolia thinks it would be fun to climb the tree with the tulips if it's okay with Aunt Astrid, but Violet doesn't want to. There is also a certain cat Magnolia thinks needs a home that she would like to try and catch—she could get her picnic basket

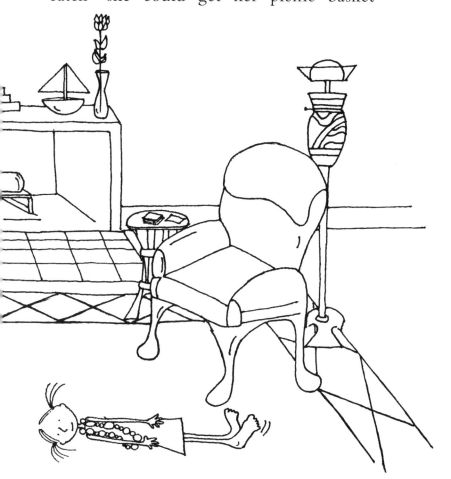

first—but Violet says, "I don't have time."

Magnolia says, "How come?"

This question makes Violet uncomfortable.

"Maybe tomorrow we could meet at the Beech Tree—that's halfway between my house and yours. And you could bring the Dog."

Violet hesitates.

"Do you want to meet halfway? We could ride bikes."

"No," says Violet uncertainly.

And although lunch is still some time away, Violet thinks she should probably start getting ready for it, or something.

"Maybe we can play another time," suggests Magnolia.

But before Violet can say "no"

or "I don't have time," Magnolia continues, "Are you really busy—is *that* why you don't have time?"

"Yes," says Violet.

"Oh," Magnolia says, turning to leave. "Well, bye, V. Bing—maybe I'll see you later."

Violet says, "Good-bye," and closes the door. In this case the truth was not so long; she just couldn't say it. For a moment, she considers trying to make herself really busy but then decides against it. For even if she were to fill her day with many things to do, she knows it still wouldn't be the truth.

* 7 *

The Best and the Worst Room

The next day, Violet forgets to put an *X* on her calendar. She is out walking the Dog with a piece of old clothesline she found in the drawer Aunt Astrid told her to look in. He doesn't seem to mind, although Violet is not sure it is the nicest thing to do to someone. She is also uncertain because she has been warned about ropes and necks and the possible *dangers*. But in this case, it seems, the Dog will be fine.

They turn the corner and come around to the side yard, walking past the tree and the bench, the tulips and bushes, and then around to the back and so forth. They circle the house. Just as they are coming around again, something catches the Dog's attention.

"What do you see?" asks Violet.

Soon she figures out that the Dog is watching a spider whose web stretches from the bush with those small red berries—which you shouldn't even try to eat—to the side of The Grand House. This is not as interesting to Violet as it is to the Dog. When Violet feels tired of the walk, they go inside. At noon, they lunch together, and in the *after*noon, they look

52

out the window in the Yellow Room. They do this every day, the same way, for quite a while, even the part where the Dog looks at the Spider, as the Spider can always be found in the same place. And at night, the Dog sleeps with Violet on the big yellow bed, although she loses him in the comforter sometimes and worries that he will suffocate. But he does not.

One day, the Dog is not in the usual places, and Violet finds him in the hallway instead.

"Hey, don't you want to go for a walk?" she asks.

But he runs away, and Violet runs after him. He runs up the stairs, and she runs up the stairs. And when he goes through the door marked BACK STAIRS TO THE FOURTH FLOOR, she follows. The Dog stops in front of two large wooden doors. One door is partly open, and he runs through. Violet walks in slowly and looks around.

The room is dirty and all the broken, peeling, unpainted, and torn things make it gloomy. It is, for certain, the worst room she has ever seen. There are many large windows, each very worn, some cracked. Grimy walls, parts and pieces on the floor, nails here and there—which as we all know, is a danger, especially to children with bare feet—peeling windowsills, rotting parts and pieces, and so much dust Violet feels sure she might sneeze, but does not. Just then, Aunt Astrid walks in.

"Oh, you found the Sunroom."

"Everything looks like it's trying to take itself down," says Violet.

"Yes, well, it is both the Best and the Worst

BACK STAIRS
TO THE
FOURTH FLOOR

Room. What it once was, it no longer is, and it is now in need of a great deal of help. Perhaps *you* can help it. All the *other* rooms have already been cleaned up, painted, and papered. They've got their furniture and rugs, pictures and plants already arranged. But *this* room could be for you to decide."

Violet shakes her head. "I don't have time."

But then she remembers this is not actually true.

"Make things the way you want them to be. You are welcome to anything you find."

The Dog runs around the room excitedly.

"I don't know why he likes it," says Violet.

"Well, there is a lot to be done here, and this room is the highest in the house. You can see so much. Look—there's the Beech Tree."

Violet looks out. Halfway doesn't seem all that far. She thinks of Magnolia and her four good names.

* 8 *
Shoes

Every day after this, whenever Violet doesn't know where the Dog is, he is in the Sunroom. Gradually she spends more time there, as well. There are six windows—five more than in the Yellow Room. And although there are some broken things, there are not as many as she'd first thought. Most of the furniture is still together, covered with canvas tarps, which she has taken to removing.

There are chairs that look like teacups, a globe, an old record player, a rug she manages to unroll, and lamps, as well—one that stands and one that sits. There is also an old bed that looks a lot like one she saw in a museum once except that at the museum, there was a velvet rope around it, so you had to walk past without touching anything—even though you'd paid to get in—which didn't seem all that fair.

Violet does her best to arrange things and, with Magnolia in mind, attempts to push the bed under one of the windows. It is quite heavy, however, so she must leave it where it is. But there are still other things to arrange, and she finds herself wondering if she might be able to paint this room herself sometime, just as Magnolia did.

There is also the Closet, which she can

walk into, filled mostly with clothing. When Violet thinks of her clothes, she thinks they must not be itchy or tucked in, overly bright, flowered, striped, polka-dotted, or tied with a bow. There are to be no tights, and certainly no stiff shoes. Violet glances at herself in the big mirror on the Closet door. She looks the same. If she *did* like to dress up, she might try on some of the dresses, gloves, and scarves. But she already knows she doesn't like to dress up and so does not.

But when she finds a shoe box with girls'-size patent-leather Mary Janes inside, she looks at them for quite a while and closes the box, but does not put it away. After several minutes, she unties her sneakers, sets them aside, opens the box, takes the SHOES out, and puts them on. She feels different with these SHOES—possibly different enough for a new name. Hesitating, she looks in the mirror again.

"Julia?" she tries. "Chris? Grace? Liz?"

She walks around the Sunroom, and around again. They are a little big, but she does not care. And from that time forward, Violet wears the SHOES all the time, taking them off only before bed or a bath, until the day something unexpected happens.

* 9 *
Something of Interest

On this day, Violet awakens and the Dog is not on her bed. Putting on her SHOES, she goes up to the Sunroom. He is not there. She looks for him all over the house and out in the yard. And when she stops at the bush with those red berries, he isn't there either, and neither is the Spider—which she takes as a very bad sign.

"Where *are* you?" she calls with a cracking voice.

Violet circles the yard again and again, walks along the path and back through the house. Astrid drives around and looks for the Dog, as well, but with no luck. It is a day spent thinking of how the Dog is not there. Up and down the stairs, in and out of every room, slamming every door to every closet, opening every drawer, Violet storms through the

house. Eventually, she races back up to the Fourth Floor, pulls the SHOES from her feet,

and throws them into the Sunroom, slamming the door as she leaves.

*   *   *

Here is Violet back in the Yellow Room, sitting in the yellow chair, looking out the window, alone. Here is the old piece of clothesline.

Aunt Astrid comes in and joins her.

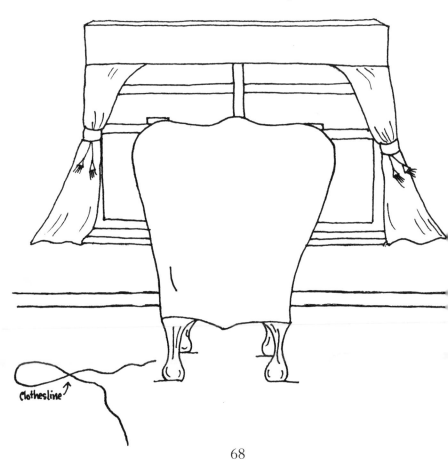

Clothesline

"You know, Violet, the Sunroom is already much improved by what you have done. I think it's well on its way to becoming the Best Room again."

Violet finds it hard to talk right now; she's still thinking about the Dog. Her throat is a little clogged.

"And there are many Things of Interest in there—I know, because once they were mine."

Violet didn't know this but nods without saying anything. After a moment, she manages some choked words.

"There's nothing I'm interested in."

But she knows this is not the truth. The truth, she thinks, is more like this: "I don't want to be interested in anything right now, Aunt Astrid, because I am busy being unhappy, and the two things just don't go together."

Astrid is silent for a moment. Getting up, she leaves the room, and when she returns, she is carrying a large bag.

"This is my old CARPETBAG," she says. "I'd like you to have it just in case."

Violet looks at her. "In case of what?"

"In case you're interested."

Setting the bag down, she hugs Violet and leaves.

Now when Violet stares out the window, she thinks of the Dog but also of that *bag*. She pushes the bag away from her with the side of her foot, and then once more, and once more again, and the last time, with a bit of a kick. She gets up, climbs into bed, and, thinking only of what she is missing, falls asleep exhausted.

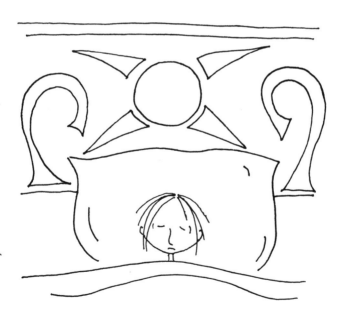

* 10 *
The Book

Now it is late and all those who should be asleep are. *not*. After a day spent napping and scarcely eating, Violet rolls onto one side, then the other, pushes off the blankets, then pulls them back. She huffs and sighs and, now and again, lets out some short, angry words. Here she is sitting up, staring out into the dark room.

Getting out of bed, she paces back and

forth, sometimes stopping to look out the window for the Dog. But it is dark and she can't see much. After a while, her attention falls on the CARPETBAG. Finally she unbuckles the straps, opens it, and pours the contents out.

There is an old-fashioned flashlight, which she considers good; knitting needles, a comb, a pencil, a handkerchief, and a yo-yo, which she considers okay; a compass, which she  does not really understand; and binoculars, which she doesn't believe are working properly. There is also a hat, a rolled-up piece of paper, and a BOOK. That's it.

She decides to look at the BOOK. Usually, she would avoid a book because books tend to take so much time. But this book seems different. Its cover is leather and soft, the pages are yellowed, and all the words are handwritten. Opening to the first page, Violet settles back into bed and begins to read.

Dedication:

For those who don't get out much
but who really ought.

Tuesday

Today was moving day. And now, here I am. There is so much I want to do, but this place is so overly big, overly confusing, overly everything—with its dusty, creaky, empty rooms. I despise it here. All the games are boring—even hopscotch—and I can't take out my new red bicycle (I just got) because I don't know my way around. There is not one thing I like (except for the Ocean, which is fairly near). This house is supposed to be so great but I don't see it at all. Now I'm off to hate it some more, I suppose.

Yours Trapped Without Good News,
A. A. Bing

"How can something be 'overly everything'? It doesn't make any sense. And hop-scotch is the same wherever you play it," says Violet.

Arranging her pillow, she makes herself more comfortable and turns the page.

Wednesday

The Ocean is the greatest place a person can go. I would not wish for even the most horrible person in the world to never get to see the Ocean, for I believe it is <u>filled</u> with hope. And yet, I still have not gotten to go. This has been the longest week, days, hours, minutes, seconds ever. I think this house has it in for me. There is nothing to do, no one to play with, nothing good at all. Every day I wish I were somewhere else—doing great things and having great talks.

Yours Without Greatness,
A. A. Bing

Violet shifts a little. "She complains a lot. And how can a house have it in for you?"

Thursday

We cannot go to the Ocean (again), and it is all I wanted to do.

Even though the beach seems close on a map, my parents say we have too many things to do today. And so, it is a day I am to do all the things I do not want to do and none of the things I want to. I don't think I need to write of how I feel about this. It is a jail of a day.

Yours Drained of All Hope and Light,
· A. A. Bing

Friday

Today—not much better, although the house
is starting to fix up, and I suggested we
make each bedroom a different color. The
bigger rooms will all be filled with whatever
interests us. So that's not all bad. And
I chose my room. It's on the fourth
floor and is filled with windows. I got a
flashlight for my bicycle, some binoculars,
and I found an old compass, and have
started to explore. Now I know every
nook of this place and hope soon to make
a map of it all. It has turned out to
be more grand than I'd thought. And I
have made a plan not to be so angry and
mean anymore but to be chipper like the
girl at school whom I don't know but
whose pretty hair I admire. I am a
grump up against one like her, and wonder

how anyone can ever stand me. And so I
will try to change.

Yours with the Usual Hair, but a
Glimmer of Hope,
A. A. Bing

Tuesday
Today, I made a MAP. I've written down
everything I've seen and can remember. I
even found a Secret Passage. Although it

is too secret to tell of, I can certainly record that I will go again soon. (Note: I have marked it "S.P." on the MAP.) With my MAP, flashlight, compass, and binoculars, I want to go everywhere and tell of where I have been. So I hereby promise to always keep record of the most faraway and nearby places I go.

Yours, Finally, with Interest and My Traveling Hat On,
Astrid Astoria Bing,
Age 9

P.S. We are going to the Ocean tomorrow! I have been promised.

Setting the book down, Violet picks up and unrolls the piece of paper. It is the MAP.

On one side, it shows all the rooms of The Grand House, and on the other, all the places *around* The Grand House. There's the path,

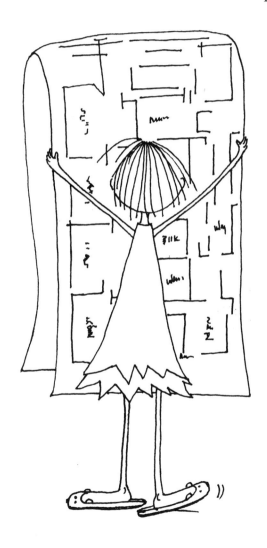

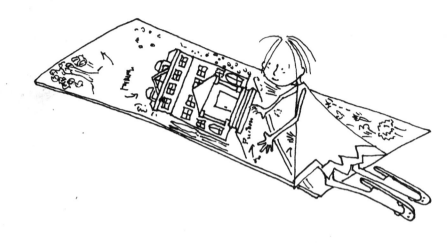

as well as the stone road that leads to the Beech Tree, to the Ocean, and as far as the City. Violet walks her fingers from The Grand House to the Beech Tree, measures the distance, and tries to imagine where Magnolia's house might be.

And inside The Grand House, every room is clearly marked, as well. Violet looks for the initials S.P. and finally finds them, faintly written, in the Closet of the Sunroom, with a line drawn extending all the way down to the Basement.

"Oh, it's in the *Sunroom*," she says thoughtfully.

* 11 *
Untrustworthy Doors

With the CARPETBAG in one hand
and the flashlight in the other, Violet is on
her way up to the Fourth Floor. She wants
her SHOES back and maybe, even, to see the
Secret Passage. Hurriedly she makes her way
to the two large wooden doors and reaches
for the handle. But they are locked.

"What?! Why have a door that

locks when nobody knows it's going to? I hate this," she says. *"I hate this!"*

Although it seems like she *should* hate this, somehow saying she hates it doesn't seem true.

It is true that this is not what she wants, but *hate* seems too strong. Just then, the expression "When the going gets tough, the tough get going" comes to mind.

"When the going gets tough," says Violet, "I always just want to go home."

But she doesn't want to go home. Opening the CARPETBAG, she takes out the MAP and looks, once more, at the Secret Passage marked in the Sunroom Closet.

"If I can get to the Basement from the Sunroom, I must be able to get to the Sunroom from the Basement," she concludes nervously.

Holding the flashlight, Violet stares out into the dark hallway before her. Moments later, she

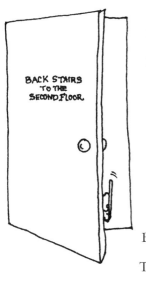

is through the door marked BACK STAIRS TO THE THIRD FLOOR and then down again and down again to the Second Floor, passing room after room. Arriving at the door marked BACK STAIRS TO THE FIRST FLOOR,

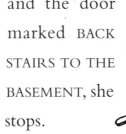

hurrying toward the Kitchen and the door marked BACK STAIRS TO THE BASEMENT, she stops.

Violet opens the door and peers down the dark steps.

"There must be a light

somewhere," she says. "Every room has a light."

Despite creaking and dark areas beyond the reach of the flashlight, she grips the railing to begin. "Just because I'm afraid doesn't mean there's anything to be afraid of."

Once down, she spots an old bulb with a hanging metal chain. When the light goes on, her attention is immediately drawn to the red BICYCLE. For the moment, Violet sets aside looking for the Secret Passage and goes over to the bike. She rolls it out, swings her leg over, and sits down. With her toes just touching the floor, the BICYCLE seems to hold her, and she wishes she could start pedaling *now* and ride. For a while, Violet forgets she is alone in a basement late at night.

After a few minutes, she carefully puts the BICYCLE back. It is then that she notices a very small door. Looking at the MAP, she recognizes it as the Secret Passage and goes over. Although the door seems to have no handle, Violet soon finds a ring that turns,

and when it turns, the door slides open.

"Oh," she says, "a *secret* handle!"

It will be a tight squeeze through a small space. Violet thinks. She would rather *not* crawl in but holds in mind that she can always crawl back out. Once through, she faces a brick wall with a heavy, iron ladder, and hesitates. There is no way to see where the ladder leads. Taking a deep breath, she decides to start climbing. The climb, though, is not easy, and carrying the CARPET-

BAG makes it all the more difficult. After a while, she realizes she does not like being up so high and thinks of the girl down the street who fell from a tree and when she landed her foot was facing the wrong way.

"I don't want my foot to face the wrong way," Violet says quietly.

She takes another deep breath and continues up another rung.

"Just go faster, Violet," she says sternly.

Another rung, another breath, and Violet is not feeling so good. She finds herself thinking that if she had a different name, she would probably be okay with climbing.

Suddenly she stops, out of breath and anxious.

"My foot is not facing the wrong way," she states firmly, trying to calm herself, "and I don't have to go faster and there is nothing wrong with the name 'Violet' for climbing."

Slowly and steadily now, she takes rung after rung and step after step, thinking only

of what she is doing. After a short time, it's up one more rung and the climbing is over. When the ladder ends, she reaches another small door. Pushing

92

on it, Violet opens the door and crawls into the Sunroom Closet.

Still a little shaken, she walks to the Sunroom, picks up her SHOES, puts them on, climbs onto the old bed, and falls fast asleep.

* 12 *
The Truth about Hats

When Violet finally awakens late the
next morning, overtired, the day still feels like
the night, and eating breakfast seems all wrong.
Instead, she stands at the Sunroom windows,
wearing her nightgown and SHOES, looking
out. She thinks about the Secret Passage, how
far she climbed, about sleeping in the old bed,
and about painting the Sunroom and what

color she might like. So when she notices something off in the distance, it does not capture her attention immediately. But after a few minutes, Violet watches more intently as whatever or whoever continues along the stone road, until finally she realizes that there in the distance, carrying Magnolia's old picnic basket in his mouth, is the Dog!

Scrambling to the door, down the hall, around the corner, down the stairs, and down again and down again, flight after flight, she finally reaches the front door and throws it open. There is the Dog. Violet takes the

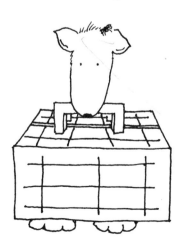

basket from his mouth and hugs him. When she lets go, she notices a spider on his ear and stops herself from brushing it off.

"Is she the one from the bush—are you friends?" she asks.

Violet likes the idea of being friends with a spider, as most people are not. Then she opens the basket. Inside is Magnolia's long strand of beads.

Followed by the Dog and the Spider, Violet carries the BEADS and the basket up to the Sunroom. The Spider im-

mediately takes to spinning a web above one of the windows while the Dog looks on.

"What a great thing," comments Violet, "to always make a home wherever you are."

Then she looks out the window at the Beech Tree.

Just then, Aunt Astrid comes in, having seen everything and followed Violet upstairs. She is very glad to see the Dog and the BEADS.

Picking up the binoculars, she hands them to Violet.

"Look through these," she says, "and see all the places you have been choosing *not* to go. Today, *go* to one of those places."

After a while, Violet sits down with a piece of paper and a pencil and writes the following note:

Dear Magnolia Greene Gold,
Do you want to meet halfway today?

Yours in beads,
V. Bing

And then she puts the BEADS around her neck, tucks the note back into the basket, and has the Dog bring it back to Magnolia.

The Dog makes a quick return with a message that says only this:

YES, V. BiNG! AT NOoN!

After dressing quickly, Violet runs downstairs, disappears into the Basement, and returns, after much effort, carrying the BICYCLE.

It is a morning spent falling, but also riding. And then falling a little less, riding a little more, and then finally, hardly falling and mostly riding, until Violet feels fairly certain she knows how to ride and what to do when she falls.

Then, using bread that is more brown than white, not as soft as she would like, and jelly with pieces of strawberries in it because there simply is *no* grape, Violet makes sandwiches, which she places in the picnic basket. Then she puts the picnic basket on the back of her bike, reaches into the CARPETBAG, removes the hat, and puts it on. Whatever the truth is about hats, she will wear it.

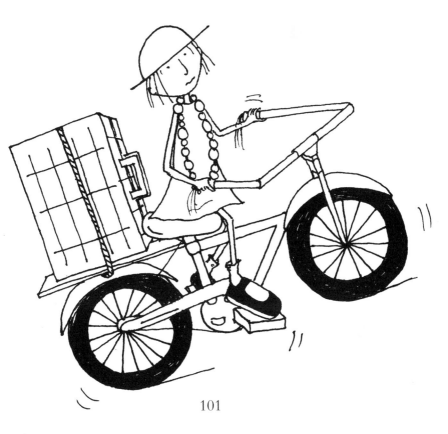

* 13 *
Meeting Halfway

On a day that feels different from any other day, Violet Bing meets Magnolia Greene Gold at the Beech Tree and they play. When they are hungry, they eat the sandwiches, which are good. And when they get tired, they lie around and talk, and when they get restless, they return to The Grand House.

Violet shows Magnolia the Sunroom, and together they decide to paint it yellow, which is not too bright. The day is long, but goes fast, which is just what you would want, and

what you get when your day is full of things you like and are interested in. When the day is done, Violet records everything in the leather BOOK she now calls *The Sunroom Stories*.

When it is time to go home, the Dog comes, too. Violet packs the BOOK and wears the BEADS. The car ride home is long but good, as her parents like the BEADS and are glad to meet the Dog. Violet looks out the window and thinks of returning to The Grand House next summer, ready to keep an eye out for Things of Interest and ready also to find out what happens next.

50